Sydney Bunny
Learns to Tie

Nathan,
Let Sydney
and Nathan
Bunny help you
learn to tie your
shoes!

You can do it "our" Nathan Bunny!

Deborah Schnell
2/2016

Written by Deborah Schnell
Illustrated by Joseph Necci

Published by:

FriesenPress
Suite 300 – 852 Fort Street
Victoria, BC, Canada V8W 1H8

www.friesenpress.com

Distributed to the trade by The Ingram Book Company

Introduction

This book was designed to help your child learn to tie their shoes. A child learns and remembers if they can relate to something familiar to them. The story is told on the pages on the left hand side and the directions are given on the pages on the right hand side. The instructions are for the adult and you should relate it to the story. The adult should say things like, "*This is the part of the story when Nathan went into the back door.*" The child will remember the story and will remember how to tie by retelling the story to themselves. A little time and patience and your child will master the art of tying in a day or two. As a teacher of 30+ years, I have consistently used this same story and have successfully taught countless children to tie within a matter of days.

In the beginning, read the entire story two to three times before trying to teach your child to tie. This will allow your child to better relate to the story as they learn to tie. Then as you are showing them how to tie, be sure to sit beside your child so they are not looking at the shoe backwards. You should demonstrate each step one or two times and then let them try it. It is easier to work with the shoe off the child's foot. Make sure the laces are not too short as this makes it much more difficult for the child.

Thank you to my wonderful family for their love and support.

To my sweet grandchildren
Sydney and Nathan

D.S.

To my beautiful wife

J.N.

Sydney Bunny and Nathan Bunny were good friends and would play together in the woods each day.

Nathan loved to play in the dirt and often got his feet dirty. Because his feet were dirty, his mother made him always come in the back door. Nathan loved it because the back door was special. It was made from two trees that had fallen into each other.

Hold both shoelaces straight up as if they were two tall trees standing in the forest. Explain to the child as you go through the steps what part of the story this step would relate to. For example: this part relates to Sydney and Nathan playing in the forest.

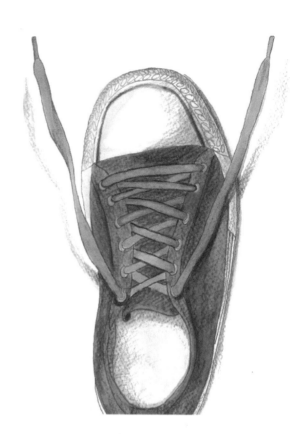

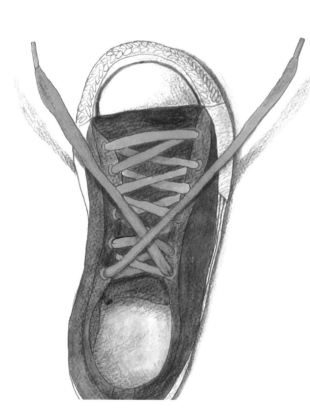

Now as if the trees fell together, cross the laces and show the child how the bottom part of the X would represent Nathan's back door.

Each time he went home, Nathan would run around the big tree and into the back door. As soon as he was inside, he would close the door tight.

At this point show them how to hold the middle of the X with your left hand and put the lace into the back of the X. Nathan Bunny represents the lace on the right with the bottom part of the X being the back door.

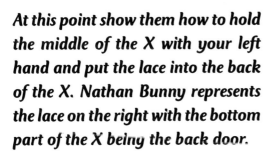

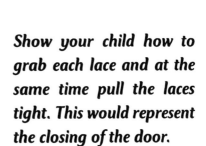

Show your child how to grab each lace and at the same time pull the laces tight. This would represent the closing of the door.

7

Sydney and Nathan's mothers would remind them to watch out for the fox and if they saw him, run home as quickly as possible. Now Sydney lived near a very large tree with roots that went deep into the ground.

One day, Sydney was outside playing when she saw a bushy red thing in the brush and thought it was the fox. She remembered what her mother had told her and quickly ran home.

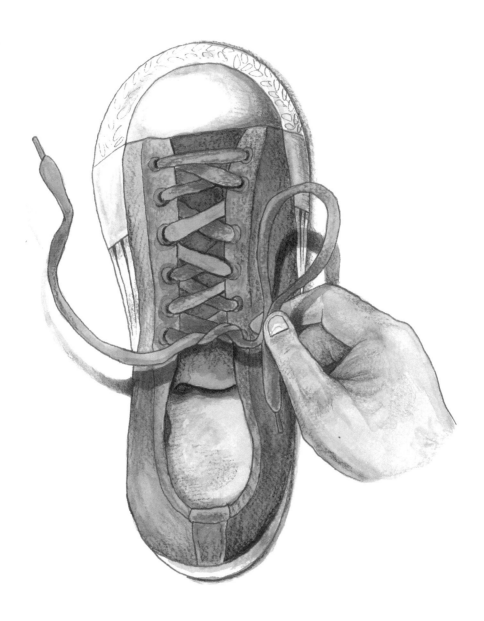

Form the loop on the right of the shoe which would represent the tree that Sydney lives in. Point out to the child that the end of the lace hangs down next to the shoe and tell them this is the root deep in the ground. Explain that a tree always grows out of the ground. This teaches the child to make the loop close to the shoe and not way above it. It doesn't matter if the child is right or left-handed, they will still do it this way without a problem.

Sydney would run around the tree in order to see the hole she must go down.

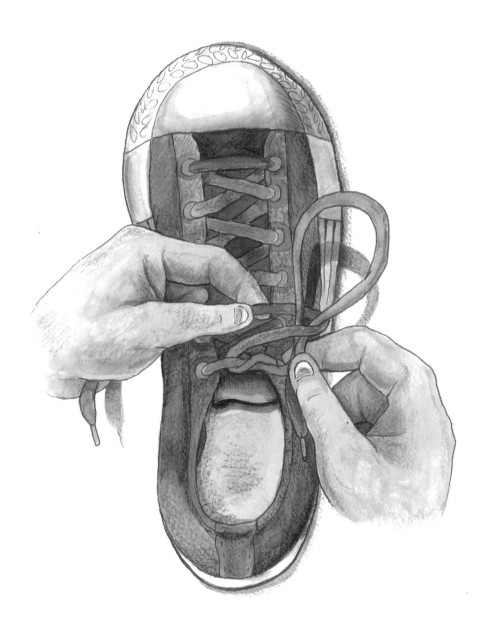

When showing the child how to wrap the lace around the loop, make sure you are wrapping counter-clockwise because this leaves the lace at the inner side of the shoe. Discuss how you can now see the hole which is on the left side of the loop. This represents how Sydney Bunny runs around the tree to go home. This also leaves their left hand free to push the lace down the hole as shown in the later illustration.

She had learned never to go into the hole head first because something could grab her tail.

This step will show your child how they should not put the end of the lace down the hole first. I guarantee they will try to do this. Explain that this is where the fox could grab her tail. Don't spend a lot of time on this. It is just a step that must be covered or they will be creating knots instead of bows. If they forget and begin to put the tip down first, just make the motion with your hand (like a pinch) and tell them, "The fox will grab her tail!"

So Sydney went down into her hole next to the tree tail first. This way she could see if anything was around.

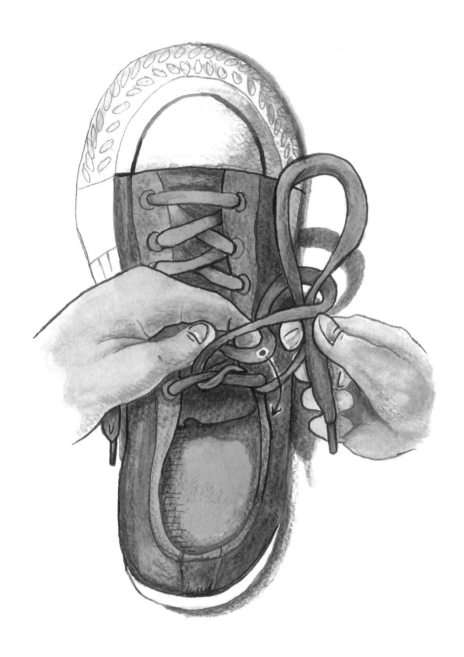

Show your child approximately where the tail would be on the lace (you could even make a small dot to represent the tail about 5-6 inches from the tip of the lace). Show them by taking your pointer finger you can push the lace down in the hole. As they are pushing the lace down the hole, make sure they do not let go of the loop.

She would often call to her mother and her mother would help by pulling her into the hole. Then they would slowly close the door to the rabbit hole and everyone was safe and happy.

This step should be taken slowly because it is difficult for the child to grasp the concept but once it is understood, they will have no problem. Demonstrate this a few times for the child. The right hand lets go of the loop and grabs the lace in the hole. The right hand would represent the mother helping Sydney. The left hand now grabs the top of the looped lace which would be the tree. Then pull both laces at the same time very slowly until they understand that pulling with one hand can pull the lace right through, resulting with only one loop.

"You did it and I'm so proud of you." said Sydney's mom. She gave her two thumbs up.

Children have a very hard time tightening their laces. They should place a thumb in each loop which is represented by mommy rabbit giving Sydney two thumbs up. Then show them how to wrap their fingers around their thumbs to make a fist and pull their laces tight.

Your child has now tied their own shoe. Congratulations!

About the Author

Deborah Schnell presently resides in a small town south of Buffalo, New York. She and her husband Ron have been married for 39 years and have two children, Brandy and Ryan and two beautiful grandchildren, Sydney and Nathan.

She recently retired after 33 years of teaching. Her first 10 years were spent in special education where she worked with children having a wide range of different disabilities. She then transferred to Kindergarten for the next 18 years and finished the remainder of her career teaching primary grades up to fourth.

She has had a desire to write children's books for a number of years and through the encouragement of many of her colleagues, family and friends, she has begun the dream.